PETER FORSBERG

MARC TARDIF

MILAN HEJDUK

PETER STASTNY

PATRICK ROY

MICHEL GOULET

DALE HUNTER

JOE SAKIC

MATS SUNDIN

REAL CLOUTIER

ADAM FOOTE

ANTON STASTNY

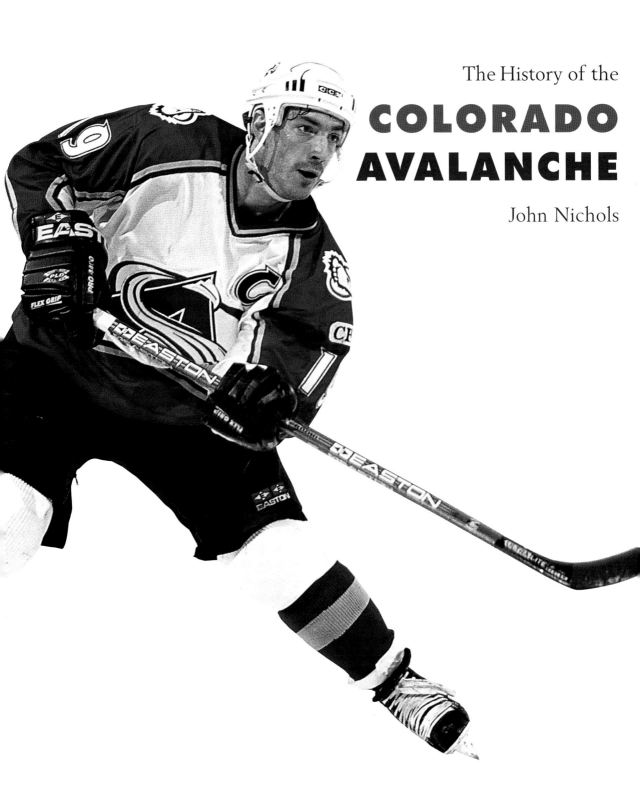

The History of the

COLORADO
AVALANCHE

John Nichols

CREATIVE C EDUCATION

Published by Creative Education, 123 South Broad Street, Mankato, MN 56001

Creative Education is an imprint of The Creative Company.

Designed by Rita Marshall.

Photographs by Getty Images (Elsa/NHLI, Tom Pidgeon/NHLI, Rick Stewart/Allsport), Hockey Hall

of Fame (Paul Bereswill, London Life-Portnoy, O-Pee-Chee), Icon Sports Media Inc. (Robert Beck),

Sports Gallery Inc. (Al Messerschmidt), SportsChrome USA (Gregg Forwerck, Layne Murdoch)

Library of Congress Cataloging-in-Publication Data

Nichols, John, 1966– The history of the Colorado Avalanche / by John Nichols.

p. cm. — (Stanley Cup champions)   ISBN 1-58341-277-8

Summary: Provides an overview of the history and key personalities associated with the team

that joined the National Hockey League in 1979 as the Quebec Nordiques but won

the Stanley Cup after moving to Denver in 1995.

1. Colorado Avalanche (Hockey team)—Juvenile literature.

[1. Colorado Avalanche (Hockey team)—History. 2. Quebec Nordiques (Hockey team)—History.

3. Hockey—History.] I. Title. II. Series (Mankato, Minn.).

GV848.C65 N53 2003   796.962'092—dc21   2002035131

First Edition 9 8 7 6 5 4 3 2 1

THE CITY OF DENVER, NESTLED IN THE FOOTHILLS OF THE ROCKY MOUNTAINS, IS COLORADO'S CAPITAL AND LARGEST CITY. NICKNAMED THE "MILE HIGH CITY" because of its lofty altitude, Denver was originally settled in the 1850s by gold seekers heading west. Since those days, the city has become a major metropolis with a population of more than two and a half million people.

The people of Denver enjoy snowy winters and the activities that go along with them—skiing, skating, and sledding. In 1995, Coloradans embraced a new winter pastime when the Quebec Nordiques of the National Hockey League (NHL) relocated to Denver and became the Colorado Avalanche. In Colorado, the club soon began rolling over opponents like the thundering wall of mountain snow for which it is named.

ANDRE GAUDETTE

{A WORLDLY BEGINNING} The Quebec Nordiques got their start in the World Hockey Association (WHA)—a rival league of the NHL—in 1972. A group of Quebec businessmen bought the struggling WHA franchise in San Francisco for $215,000 and moved it to Quebec. The new ownership group called the team the Nordiques (French for "northerners"), and the franchise began play in 1972–73.

Quebec's J.C. Tremblay was named the WHA's best defenseman in both **1972–73** and **1974–75**.

The Nordiques' first two seasons were marked by coaching changes and a lot of losses, but by 1974–75, Quebec was on the rise. A midseason trade with the Michigan Stags brought over high-scoring wing Marc Tardif, and his 38 goals in 53 games propelled the Nordiques to a division title. Quebec advanced to the WHA championship series but lost to the Houston Aeros and their star, hockey legend Gordie Howe.

MARC TARDIF

Star wing Real Cloutier was the WHA's top goal scorer in **1976–77** and **1978–79**.

REAL CLOUTIER

In 1976–77, Tardif and fellow sharp-shooting winger Real Cloutier helped Quebec return to the finals. This time it faced the Winnipeg Jets. The series was a tough battle that went seven hard-hitting games, but in the end, the Nordiques prevailed and claimed the WHA championship. "I'm really proud that we didn't let last year's championship loss get in our heads," said Cloutier. "Last year we were good, but this year we were great."

Winger Serge Bernier helped the **1976–77** Nordiques set a WHA record with 60 victories.

Quebec remained a strong team as the '70s wore on, but the WHA began to falter financially. The league had several well-managed clubs, but several others were losing money at an alarming rate. Talks began with the more established NHL, and on March 30, 1979, an agreement was reached. The WHA would fold, but the league's four financially sound teams would join the ranks of the NHL. The surviving teams were the Edmonton Oilers, Hartford

SERGE BERNIER

Quebec's history of outstanding defensemen includes **1990s** star Curtis Leschyshyn.

C. LESCHYSHYN

Whalers, Winnipeg Jets, and Quebec Nordiques.

{THE STASTNY BROTHERS ARRIVE} Although there was a

Quebec's **1982–83** squad netted a whopping 360 goals, setting a club record that still stands.

lot of excitement in Quebec over the Nordiques' new NHL status, the club's first season was a disappointment. With only 25 wins in 80 games in 1979–80, it was obvious some rebuilding was necessary.

Quebec scored a major coup in its search for talent when the team signed brothers Peter and Anton Stastny. The speedy forwards had spent the early part of their careers playing in Czechoslovakia, a country under the control of the former Soviet Union. At the time, it was extremely difficult for players from communist nations to get permission to leave their countries. Soon, a third Stastny forward—older brother Marian—joined the team as well. The Stastnys' move paved the way for a long line of great eastern European talents to play in North America.

THE STASTNYS

With the Stastnys added to a lineup that already featured

Cloutier, Tardif, and hard-shooting wing Michel Goulet, the

Nordiques were among the league's best offensive teams in the

early 1980s. The Stastnys consistently combined for more than 100

goals and 170 assists, while Goulet blossomed into one of the NHL's

great scorers, netting 50 or more goals a year every season from

1982–83 to 1985–86. "They come at you in waves," said Boston

Bruins defenseman Brad Park. "They are all so quick and good with

the puck. Throw in Goulet and there may as well be

four brothers."

Michel Goulet, Peter Stastny, and Marian Stastny represented Quebec in the **1983** All-Star Game.

Although Quebec was a scoring machine, the team

gave up goals as easily as it scored them. The Nordiques

had great speed and skill, but—with the exception of

rough-and-tumble center Dale Hunter—they lacked size and

toughness. Nowhere was this shortcoming more apparent than in the

playoffs. NHL postseason games tend to be played with plenty of

hard checking and grinding defense. More often than not, the

Nordiques' high-flying style crashed in the playoffs.

The high points for the Nordiques of the early '80s were the

1982 and 1985 playoffs. Coming off a 30–32–18 regular season, the

Nordiques barely made the 1982 playoffs. After upsetting Montreal

MICHEL GOULET

in the first round, Quebec continued its dream season by defeating

Boston in the second round. In the Eastern Conference Finals,

however, the New York Islanders rolled over Quebec in a four-game

sweep. In 1985, Quebec earned playoff victories over Buffalo and

Montreal before being bounced from the conference finals in six

games by the Philadelphia Flyers.

{QUEBEC FALLS AND RISES} As the 1980s wore on, Quebec's fortunes began to slide. Marian Stastny left the team in 1985, and although Peter and Anton were still productive, they could not carry the load themselves. In 1986–87, the Nordiques suffered the first of six straight losing seasons.

Looking to rebuild, Quebec's front office began to trade the team's veterans for younger players. In 1987, Dale Hunter and goalie Clint Malarchuk were dealt to the Washington Capitals for two players and a draft pick that would be used to select center Joe Sakic. By 1990, Goulet and the Stastnys were also gone.

The bright side to Quebec's losing ways was that the team consistently got high picks in the NHL Draft. In 1989 and 1990, the team drafted high-scoring center Mats Sundin, defenseman Adam Foote, and rugged wing Owen Nolan. And in 1991, the team

Tough guy Dale Hunter led the team in penalty minutes for six straight seasons in the **1980s**.

DALE HUNTER

Players such
as center
Chris Drury
helped make
Colorado a
late **1990s**
powerhouse.

selected highly touted center Eric Lindros with the first overall

pick. Although Sundin, Foote, and Nolan quickly became impact

players, the draft pick that did the most to shake the

Nordiques from their losing funk was Lindros—even

though he never played a single minute for the team.

After being drafted, Lindros upset Quebec fans by

announcing that he wanted to play for a winning team

and would not sign with the Nordiques. Forced to trade him,

Quebec eventually accepted a lucrative trade offer from the

Philadelphia Flyers. In exchange for Lindros, Quebec received

All-Star goalie Ron Hextall, centers Mike Ricci and Peter Forsberg,

defensemen Steve Duchesne and Kerry Huffman, wing Chris Simon,

first-round draft picks in 1993 and 1994, and $15 million. "It was

maybe the biggest trade in hockey history," said Nordiques general

manager Pierre Page. "Eric is a great player, but we needed more

ADAM FOOTE

than one great player to turn our team around."

Over the next two seasons, the Nordiques began to improve.

Sakic, Sundin, and Nolan formed a high-scoring attack, while Foote

and fellow defenseman Alexei Gusarov cleared traffic for Hextall.

Quebec's 47–27–10 record in 1992–93 let the rest of the NHL know

that the team's days as a doormat were over.

The future looked bright for the Nordiques in the mid-1990s, as the young team was maturing and

beginning to develop a championship swagger. But off the ice, the franchise was hurting financially. Quebec had a hard time drawing fans, and because Canadian money is worth less than American money, Canadian teams had to pay more than American teams to keep

In one **1995** game, wing Claude Lemieux helped the Avs dominate the San Jose Sharks 12–2.

players. With no answer to these problems, the franchise was sold to

a new ownership group in Denver in 1995.

Renamed the Colorado Avalanche, the team got off to a hot

start in Denver. On December 5, 1995, the Avs—as their fans called

them—swung a trade that dramatically changed the course of the

franchise. Colorado sent goaltender Jocelyn Thibault and wings

Andrei Kovalenko and Martin Rucinsky to the Montreal Canadiens

for All-Star goalie Patrick Roy and winger Mike Keane.

CLAUDE LEMIEUX

No goalie in
NHL history
has played in
more playoff
games than
Patrick Roy.

PATRICK ROY

Roy had earned a reputation as the game's best big-game goalie by winning two Stanley Cups in Montreal. Supremely confident, Roy thrived on playoff pressure, and with Montreal in a rebuilding phase, the fiery goalie had grown unhappy. The trade to up-and-coming Colorado reinvigorated Roy and gave the Avs something the franchise had always lacked—a shutdown goalie who could break opponents' spirit with his spectacular saves.

Multitalented center Peter Forsberg averaged 69 assists a season from **1995–96** to **1998–99**.

With Roy minding the nets, the Colorado offense ran wild in 1995–96. The sharp-shooting Sakic poured in 51 goals, while Peter Forsberg's playmaking skills accounted for 116 points (goals plus assists). Tough wing Claude Lemieux also scored 39 goals as the Avalanche rolled to the Pacific Division title. In the postseason, Colorado rode Sakic's 17 goals to victories over the Vancouver Canucks, Chicago Blackhawks, and Detroit Red Wings.

PETER FORSBERG

In the Stanley Cup Finals, Colorado faced the Florida Panthers. The Avs beat the Panthers easily in the first three games. In game four, the Panthers stubbornly battled Colorado to a 0–0 stalemate

through regulation and two overtimes. Finally, in the third extra session, Sakic won a face-off in the Florida zone and drew the puck back to defenseman Uwe Krupp, who whistled a hard slap shot into the Florida net. At 1:05 A.M., the Avalanche gave the city of Denver its first major sports championship. "We had so many tough years in Quebec," said an exhausted Adam Foote. "But all those tough times gave us the strength to win a game like this one."

{MISSION 16W} The Avalanche remained a power in the NHL's Western Conference through the rest of the 1990s. The driving forces behind the team's winning ways were Sakic and Forsberg. The quiet Sakic had been the franchise's centerpiece since the 1988–89 season. Armed with one of the hardest and most accurate wrist shots in the game, Sakic could snap the puck into the net in the time it took opposing goalies to blink. Although a perennial All-Star, Sakic never acted like a superstar, often deferring credit to his teammates for the Avalanche's success.

Forsberg, a native of Sweden, joined the team in 1994 and

With the help of versatile wing Scott Young, Colorado hoisted its first Stanley Cup in **1996**.

SCOTT YOUNG

immediately established himself as one of the game's top all-around players. The 6-foot and 205-pound Forsberg broke the stereotype of

Wing Valeri Kamensky scored one of the Avs' two hat tricks (three-goal games) in **1997-98**.

European players as being skilled but unwilling to engage in the physical battles common in North American hockey. Often assigned to defend the opposing team's top scorer, Forsberg seemed to enjoy delivering a bone-rattling check as much as scoring a goal.

Behind their two superstars and the play of such talented youngsters as defenseman Sandis Ozolinsh and wing Milan Hejduk, the Avalanche won four straight division titles from 1996–97 to 1999–00. Three times during that stretch, Colorado reached the Western Conference Finals, only to be turned away twice by the Dallas Stars and once by the Detroit Red Wings.

Looking for a spark to get them back to the Stanley Cup Finals, the Avs traded three prospects and a draft pick for wing

V. KAMENSKY

Dave Andreychuk and All-Star defenseman Ray Bourque during the 1999–00 season. Bourque had spent 21 stellar seasons with the Boston Bruins but had never hoisted the Stanley Cup. Late in the 2000–01 season, the Avs also brought in star defenseman Rob Blake. Bourque and Blake anchored Colorado's defensive corps and increased its offensive firepower as well.

In his final NHL season, Ray Bourque made the All-Star team for the 19th consecutive season.

Heading into the 2001 postseason, Bourque gave the team its battle cry when he announced that winning the Cup was "Mission 16W," referring to the 16 total victories it would take to capture the world championship. The Avs took their mission to heart, smashing through the Vancouver Canucks, Los Angeles Kings, St. Louis Blues, and New Jersey Devils to capture their second Stanley Cup. "Watching Ray Bourque hold the Cup was something I'll never forget," said Colorado coach Bob Hartley. "I believe with him, we

RAY BOURQUE

Winner of the **2000–01** Hart Trophy, Joe Sakic was the heart of the Avs franchise.

JOE SAKIC

Quick and hard-shooting winger Milan Hejduk was a rapidly rising Colorado star.

MILAN HEJDUK

were a team of destiny."

Following the championship celebration, Bourque retired, his

With his great
size and
smart play,
Martin Skoula
was expected
to become
an elite
defenseman.

marvelous career complete. But the Avalanche moved

on, and in 2001–02, some new talent began to emerge

in support of Sakic and Forsberg. Winger Alex Tanguay

and defenseman Martin Skoula played major roles as

the Avs captured another division title. In the playoffs,

Colorado marched to the Western Conference Finals but was turned

away by Detroit in seven hard-fought games.

For more than 30 years, the Avalanche franchise has provided

thrills for hockey fans in Quebec and Denver—two cities 1,750

miles apart. Today, backed by some of the NHL's loudest and most

loyal fans, the Avs are a perennial favorite to bring home yet another

Stanley Cup. Expectations are high, but that seems only fitting for a

team in the Mile High City.

MARTIN SKOULA

LLOYD GEORGE SCHOOL,
830 PINE STREET,
KAMLOOPS, B.C.